D1376430

Memory Lane

JOHN YAMRUS

Photo Collages by Eileen Murphy
https://mishmurphy.com/

Exterior by Julie Valin
www.TheWordBoutique.net

ISBN: 978-1-926860-61-9

Epic Rites Press publications are distributed
worldwide by Tree Killer Ink. For more information
about *Memory Lane* (and other books and publications
from Epic Rites Press) please visit the Epic Rites
website at www.epicrites.org, the Tree Killer Ink
website at www.treekillerink.com, or address Tree
Killer Ink / Epic Rites Press at PO Box 80002
Woodbridge, Sherwood Park, Alberta, Canada T8A
5T4, or contact Wolfgang Carstens at
info@treekillerink.com.

Epic Rites: any press is only as "small" as its thinking.

For Wolf Carstens:
my publisher,
enabler,
and friend.

And,
of course,
for
Kathy

JUNE 1959

JUL
19

I

my sister told me one day i should write a memoir.
i don't think it's so much for what i have to say, as
much as for how i say it. she one time told me that
i write the way i talk, and she recently moved to
Albuquerque and i think she just misses hearing me
talk.

anyway, i started re-reading Virgil's *Aeneid* this
morning and his first line:

"I sing of warfare, and a man at war"

made me think of the first line of *The Lusiads* by
Luis Vaz de Camoes:

"Arms are my theme, and those matchless
heroes..."

i had to dig up my copy of *The Lusiads* to get the
quote right...but, there it was...i don't know why
and i don't know what it means...but, there it was.

and if you've never read Virgil...or Camoes...you're
missing out.

i guess i thought of it because i was thinking that if
you're going to write a memoir...or a book of any

kind, for that matter...you'd better have a really good opening line. something catchy, like:

"It was the best of times, it was the worst of times."

(Dickens always knew how to start things off!)

Or:

"It began as a mistake."

Bukowski was also no slouch when it came to knowing just how to grab a reader's attention. the point is, i figured if i was gonna sit down and write my memoir, i'd better be able to begin it in a fashion that would grab the reader by the throat and (like the blurbs on the covers always say) "send them off on a whirlwind of an adventure." so, this is the best i got...this is my beginning, and if it doesn't grab you by the throat or by anything else you've got, then you'd better close this book right now, put it back on the shelf where you found it and walk away.

here's my beginning:

i never was any good at anything but sitting down in front of a keyboard and talking about myself and i'm not really very good at that.

since memoirs deal with memory, the first real
memory i have has to do with a cookout at my
uncle and aunt's place. i've always talked about an
earlier memory...remembering where i was when
my umbilical cord fell off, but that's just bullshit,
something that's been fed into me by parents and
relatives, and memorized by me and repeated so
often that it has since become fact.
no, the first real memory i have is being at my uncle
and aunt's place for a cookout. they lived down the
street from us...just two blocks. in fact, if you stood
out in the yard you could see their house from ours.
it was a lot nicer than ours. small. built in a style
best described as Tudor.

looking at the house from the street...to the left
there was a slope that led down to the railroad
tracks. at the top of the slope at the edge of their
property was this great big willow tree, with
branches that hung down to the ground, and on
summer days when my uncle was at work, me and
my cousin—who lived next door to them—our
whole family on both sides lived really close—and
me and him would grab onto those low-hanging
willow branches and swing out over the slope,
wishing there was a pool or a pond or a lake or a
river we could let go and drop into.

i was born in 1951...most definitely a child of the
50's in every way you can imagine. in fact,

somewhere around here i have a photo of me, maybe 6 years old or so, standing in my front yard, with a fresh haircut and great big smile on my face (if you look close you can see i've got a tooth missing), posed with my fists up in the air like a boxer, like maybe Dick Tiger or Emile Griffith who i'd watch on the *Gillette Friday Night Fights*, with my father, while he and my mother sat on the couch drinking beer.

let me back up a bit here...this isn't going to be a strict memoir in the traditional sense...not by any means. my brain's not wired that way. this is gonna be more like jazz...like a conversation between instruments...each going off on its own journey...each feeding into and onto the whole, so that i may skip around a bit (maybe even a whole lot) and i may not end up exactly where i wanted to end up, but the journey getting there will hopefully be worth the effort. at least, for me, it will.

anyway, i was talking about this tree at my uncle's... this was the 50's, remember, so even though my uncle and aunt lived there, the house was always thought of and described as being my uncle's.

but, getting back to Dick Tiger and Emile Griffith...i
looked it up...the first time they fought was in 1966,
so it wasn't a 1950's memory anyway, which
should teach you something about believing what
you read in memoirs...especially this one...because
i'm looking backward now and in that looking back
i somehow still combine that tree and my memories
of Dick Tiger and Emile Griffith and my mom and
my dad and beer and the *Friday Night Fights*, so,
like i was saying, we'd swing out on that tree, over
those tracks...

and as we'd swing out, over the slope, away from
the house, toward the tracks...(i'm trying to paint
the picture here, of how the house was
situated)...off to our left, two blocks up the street,
was the house where i lived. it was gray and old
and small, with two rooms in the downstairs front,
and two front doors (don't ask me why, because we
never never never opened one of them. ever. it
was painted shut. and the paint would change
with the years, going from grey to white and back
again to grey...but whatever color it happened to
be, we never opened that door). so, now, i can get
back to me and my cousin swinging on those
willow branches, out over the slope and down
toward the tracks.

[handwritten margin note: Posir / How Life / would Have / Been if / The Doors / were Switched]

we played on and around those tracks, those summers of 6 and 7 and 8...and when a train would come, we'd all yell TRAIN! the minute we heard the whistle and we'd stand and watch while it rolled slowly by, usually boxcars filled with who knows what, going who knows where.

on those days when we had a couple of extra pennies, we'd put one or two or three or four on the tracks and wait and watch while the train passed and when it was gone we'd run down and look to find the pennies which were still hot from the passing, and they were flat and we'd talk about taking them home and saving them forever, but we never did and they're long gone and the only thing saved forever is this memory of me and them and the trains.

so, even though i'm starting to sound like a broken record (and forgive me this one final bit of digression), but why do i keep coming back to thoughts of Dick Tiger and Emile Griffith? those two who stand out in my memory in black and white like the TV we had...or, the little tiny articles they had in *TV Guide magazine* or the great and sensational cover stories in *Ring magazine*, which i would only read in the little barber shop on Miller street...a shop with just one chair and one barber

who gave haircuts to kids for 25 cents, and i was
convinced it was the only place in the whole wide
world where you could find or buy *Ring magazine*.

Tiger and Griffith being two very gifted, very tough
black men, one of whom would one day later on
have very public struggles with his sexual identity.
even though i don't know his whole story, i'm sure
he even had trouble way back in his prime, but it
was a very different world back then, and things
like that weren't really talked about, or questioned.
they just didn't exist. at least not for us. we were
just mom and dad and apple pie and cookouts on
saturday nights with the family.

we were a family of coal miners. my grandfather,
who lived across the street from us, was a coal
miner his whole life. he spoke very little english
and he'd sit in his kitchen, next to the chimney
which was warm and felt good on his tired, aging
bones, and when he wasn't in the hole working or
in the kitchen he was in church...at least that's the
way i remember him.

my grandmother was short and wore black shoes.
great big clunky black shoes, kind of like old school
high top sneakers, only leather, with block heels.
the only other people i saw who wore shoes like

that were boxers. they laced up all the way to the top and must have taken forever to put on and take off. i never saw her out of them. i never saw her barefoot. i never saw her anywhere except in church, or in the yard, or in that chair where she used to sit and pray the rosary.

my father was a coal miner. my uncles (at least those in the family who stuck around town and never moved out) were coal miners. the whole neighborhood pretty much revolved around the mines or businesses that went to somehow support the mines.

i can remember my father and my grandfather both proudly showing me their hands, black and scarred and gnarled and made them old before their time, eventually killing them, one after another.

my uncle Duke, who was throwing the party, was missing the pointer finger on his right hand. i'm told he lost his finger in the mines, when his hand was run over by a coal car, but, we were kids then and i don't really know what the real story was, but that's what we were told and we believed it.

he retired early. i don't know how old he was, but he seemed ancient. short and balding and kind of heavy, and he had asthma so bad he could never sit down and he'd stand in his parlor, behind the chair that faced the TV, near the kitchen so he could go back and forth for his beer...and he'd light his smokes with this odd and really smooth movement of his hand and it fascinated me to watch him with that missing finger of his, light the match, touch it to his cigarette and then like Jimmy Cagney, blow it out and go on talking, never missing a beat or a word or a joke, except to cough and we'd all wait while he hacked it up, then wipe his face and mouth with his handkerchief and put it back in his pocket and go on with the story or whatever it was he was saying.

from their living room where he stood, you could look out toward that willow tree and when we were done playing, swinging on the branches, if we didn't clean up the ground there would be broken branches all over the place...and, looking further to the right, from the tracks, toward the back yard, at the side of the house was a dog house where their dog Tippy lived. Tippy was a chained, vicious, angry snarling dog whose only lot in his entire sad life was to pace back and forth at the length of his chain which was maybe 15 feet long, so much walking that he'd worn out the grass and the only thing he had to walk on was beat down dirt and

scrub and once a day my uncle would come down
and feed him and change his water which was
always green and dirty and filled with mud and
bugs.

i felt sorry as hell for Tippy, but every time i went
near him to let him know how i felt, he'd strain at
the chain and bark, wanting to bite me and hate me
and everyone else who came near, for the sad, hot,
chained life he was forced to live day in and day
out.

down the street from us, halfway between the place
where my grandmother lived and the two houses
where my uncles and aunts lived, there was the ball
field where we spent our time and days. the field
was really the parking lot for the church where we
went on sundays. it was a catholic neighborhood
with churches and bars practically right on top of
each other, practically on every other block.
anyway, the ball field was paved over for the cars,
and unusable by us after dark when it was filled
with cars for the bowling alley that was on the first
floor of the building. the school took up the second
floor, and the basement was a great big hall that
was pitch dark and we'd break into it sometimes
and play hide and seek in the dark until the
custodian came and chased us out.

the field (parking lot) was used by whatever bunch
of kids who were in the right age group to inherit it
from the older kids who went on to high school and
dating and cars and whatever else it was they did,
and the younger kids who we tried to keep out
before *they* were old enough to inherit it from us.

it was a big enough lot. rectangular...and home
plate was in one corner and center field was in the
farthest corner at the opposite end. someone, years
before us, had painted on the wall of the garage
that served as center field, a great big 309 in white
letters maybe 7 or 8 inches high in white paint. that
was a pretty good poke for kids our size and age,
and we rarely hit anything that far...for two
reasons...(one) most of us were right-handed kids
who hit everything to left field, and (two) anything
hit to right was considered an automatic out, so we
all pulled the ball to left, which had a shorter
fence...an actual fence, broken here and there by the
garage where the priest kept his cars and the shed
where they kept things belonging to the church.

we were a bit older for this part of the story (the
baseball part)...maybe 9 or 10 or 11, but, i'm just
trying to fill in the picture of the whole
neighborhood where we grew up and what it was
like back then.

eventually, this will all start to make sense...or, maybe not...maybe it'll be as confused and confusing to you as it still is to me, these sixty or so years after the fact.

now, to pick up where i left off..."i"? "i"? did i say "i"? maybe i should say "we"...because like it or not, we're in this together, and if you stick with me long enough, maybe this will all make sense to the both of us.

so, continuing to look toward the right...past the tree...past Tippy the dog...toward the back yard, and even further than that; beyond the back yard, there was a large field that was a storage and supply area for a company that made material for paving the roads. if it had a name, and i'm sure it did, i never knew it. there were no signs or anything anywhere...just piles after piles of paving stones of various sizes and shapes. big stones. little stones. pebbles. stones all over the place.

the piles of stones made great places for us kids to play in.

i read somewhere once that the dream is always killed by reality. well, our reality back then *was* the dream. and we'd play all day on those piles of stones, concocting our own reality of war games and the Alamo and Davy Crockett, taking turns being the hero and the last one standing. the last one to die in whatever scenario we came up with.

beyond the stones there were a couple of buildings, where i suppose they manufactured the tar or whatever else it was they used for making the road.

next to the buildings there was a tar pit...just a puddle, really, where the run-off black sticky tar used to pool, bubbling up, hot and steamy in the summer, trapping and killing any birds or mice or squirrels unlucky enough to wander into it or try to get across.

finishing this descriptive circle around what amounted to a two house island, surrounded as it was on all sides by the street and the tree and the tracks and the tar...potential killing fields, for sure...the final side was made up of the longest, darkest, most forbidding alley that ever lived. i purposely said *lived*, because to us kids the alley *was* alive...it was filled with everything that made up our young world...all the dread and hope and fear that we lived and played and cried and ate with every single day.

across the alley was the house where Black Mary
lived. i don't remember knowing if she ever had a
name. maybe our parents knew it. maybe *theirs*
did. i just know that the only name we ever knew
her by was Black Mary.

i saw her maybe no more than a dozen times in my
life, but each time i did, she scared the living shit
out of me.

our parents had always told us that if you were
unlucky enough to run into Black Mary and she
looked you in the eye you'd turn to stone.

how could it not be true?

she was tiny, Black Mary was, but her power was
formidable. the power we kids had invested in her
was real and strong.

i don't ever remember seeing her in the daytime.

never.

not ever.

it was always at night and she was always dressed in black. completely. head to toe black, with a scarf on her head and a veil over her eyes.

when we saw her walking (always at night), we'd hide behind hedges and trees, trying to scoot down and get a look at her and understand the magic, hoping against hope that you could get a good look without her turning around and giving you the eye and turning you into stone.

Black Mary was probably an old Italian woman, widowed early, who wore black because that's just what widows wore back then. especially Italian widows. i've seen *The Godfather* several times...i know!

maybe some of the adults even knew her or talked to her or drove her back and forth from the market. she had to have had a life somewhere.

but, all we knew was that she walked the streets at night and could turn you into a dead solid block of ice cold stone with just a single look.

so, we stayed away from her.

when we rode our bikes down the alley past her house we never looked to the right.

in the winter, on our sleds, we never looked over...hung our heads and imagined what sort of fantastic unknown hells lay just behind her door.

(Note to self: my first mistake was believing the world was fair.

when we're kids, we make a lot of mistakes. when we're older we make even more.

at the end of the day, nothing's fair. not the street you live on...not the field where you play...not even the houses where you live, or the tar, or the trees. eventually, though, you move on and maybe even get to grow up and look back over your shoulder and talk about it all.)

II

we were poor, but we covered it well.
that's a lie, because i really can't say what other
people knew or felt or saw when they looked at us.
the truth is, though, we *were* poor, of a relative
kind...just not dirt poor...not Tom Joad *Grapes Of
Wrath* poor. not barefoot in the dirt all year round
poor...but, we were indeed poor.

i just didn't have a real sense of it until i had grown
up and moved away and was able to look back on
things and see them in a different light.

things always have a way of looking different when
you see them over your shoulder.

my father was a coal miner.

sure, he had other jobs...after the war was over he
had a bunch of jobs. he worked in a silk mill...he
drove a soda truck...was a handy man/gardener for
a Jewish family ("they're Jews, but, they're still *nice*
people"...) but, if i had to give one job to describe
my father...he was a coal miner.

we had a coal bin in the basement, under the porch.
there was a window at the front/center of the

house that we'd open and the delivery truck would back up as far as it could, close to the house, and the guy would connect a slide from the truck into the window and he'd dump usually two tons of coal into the basement. a big, black, wet pile of coal that my father had helped dig out of the ground.

later on, when he was older, he drove one of those trucks. i can still see him now, in his baseball cap that he used to wear when he went fishing...the cap that he'd wear slung off to the side of his head. he had style back then, my father did.

they all did.

he'd step out of that coal truck and it was like god coming down from heaven. the door would swing open and he'd step out, real slow, like a gunslinger...like Gary Cooper in *High Noon*, slow and sure and deliberate. and then he'd kinda pose...one foot in the cab...one foot on the ground...and i thought that no one ever had a dad cooler or stronger or wiser than me.

no one.

time always has a way of proving you wrong, but for those few seconds when he'd stand there outside that truck, he was the total embodiment of IT.

he was 45 when the mines killed him.

III

his heart gave out a few days after he got home
from the hospital where he was given a new valve
for a heart already worn out and grossly enlarged
from years in the mines and a bout with rheumatic
fever when he was a boy.

we found him, dead, sitting up in bed, propped
against the wall...all blue in the face, with his eyes
half open.

he must have felt something during the night and
got up either to wait it out or to call my mother, but
nothing happened. he never called, and no one
came, and he died there, leaning against the wall
like an old doll. a blue-faced doll that wasn't any
good to anyone anymore.

when he came home from the hospital, for those
few days he had left, he slept in that room, which
was my room, which was downstairs, behind the
kitchen, toward the back of the house.

right now, as i write this, i'm sitting in the sun
room...i've got a CD on and i'm listening to Lena
Horne singing *Stormy Weather*...not the one from
the 1941 movie, but the live version, from years

later...1957, after she'd put on a whole lot more miles and life had beaten her up, but not beaten her down.

this version will tear you up and break your heart.

great music and great artists will do that to you. Lena Horne...Janis Joplin...Django Reinhardt...Johnny Hodges...Billie...

Billie Holliday didn't even have to sing a single word...just take one look into her eyes...those haunted, hunted eyes...and she would break your heart.

(Note to self: This memoir is going to be difficult to keep straight...for the reader as well as the writer...because memories aren't linear (anyone who's read Proust knows that)...memories are like leaves on a tree...and they fall at different times, at different speeds, in different ways...eventually, no matter how they fall, they end up covering the ground.)

my father wasn't a big man...i think he was 5'10". he was a ballplayer and one time had a tryout with the Chicago White Sox. i can't say if he was any good or not, because he never talked about it. in fact, it was my mother (years after he died) who told me he even *had* the tryout.

i think he was a pitcher...or, maybe he was a shortstop.

those were the two positions he always groomed me for. maybe it was because he saw some talent in me for those positions...or, maybe it was because that's where he had played when he was young...or, maybe, seeing how scrawny i was that's all he figured i was good for. i'd certainly never be a home run hitter, or a star of any kind, so, maybe he knew that if he worked me hard enough and long enough he just might be able to turn me into a relief pitcher or utility player.

we'd play catch out front after he got home from work...when he wasn't too busy or too tired.

he was actually the one who taught me how to throw a curve ball. we'd stand out there, on the sidewalk in front of the house and he'd snap off these long, slow curves that seemed to start out somewhere on the porch and curve right back into my glove in great big arches.

maybe he figured that would be my only shot at the
big leagues...knowing how to throw a curve.
maybe that's what kept *him* out of the bigs, because
his curve ball didn't snap off, or "drop off the
table," like the great ones did...his started curving
and arching the minute it came out of his hand.
any good hitter could pick up the spin on
something like that and clobber the hell out of it. it
couldn't fool anybody.

there was absolutely no deception.

but, for what it was, it was one of the most
beautiful things i've ever seen.

i can still see it spinning.

i can still hear him saying "you just *snap* your
wrist...like this..." and he'd hold the ball in his hand
(great big coal miner's hand) and show me how to
let it roll over my finger.

god, that was great.

and, then...just like that, he was gone.

45 years old and we found him dead in my
room...blue in the face, eyes open and staring, with
a line of spit running down his chin.

. . .

playing catch like that...just a boy and his
dad...1950's America...whenever i dropped the ball,
or if i looked back over my shoulder, if i looked
down toward the end of the street, i could see those
two houses that belonged to my uncles and aunts.
they were there, right in my face, looking back at
me, because the road we lived on went straight
down toward their house...past my grandmother's
on the left...past the funeral home...past the church
and the ballfield on the right, ending at their
houses, where the road took a sharp turn to the
right, and if you followed that road out for a couple
of blocks, it would take you to Luzerne, which for
all the world reminded me of that town whose
name i now forget which was in that Marlon
Brando movie *The Wild One*...1954...*the* absolute
greatest motorcycle movie of all time...even though
it hasn't held up very well over the years and, truth
be told, Brando was kinda fat in it, or at least
chubby by modern anti-hero standards...but, god,
he was cool...i can still see him in that opening
scene where he's just pulled into town, and he's got

on these really neat silvered sunglasses and he takes them off and squints in the way we all wanted to squint back then, because we all wanted to be young and tough and cool like Brando, and there was that way he had of acting, which i guess was part of *the method,* that made everything he did seem absolutely perfect and natural, and when he took off his glasses, he wiped off a bit of dust and ran it around between his fingers...he was wearing black leather gloves and i wanted gloves like that, but the only kind i ever had were orange calf-skin that were nice, but nothing cool and black and soft like the kind Marlon Brando had.

(Note to self: It takes a lot of nerve to write a memoir. Some people may even call it arrogance. I have neither. I'm writing this just to remember the people I knew as a kid. Like it or not—whether they knew it or not—they helped make me into whatever kind of a man I am today. They deserve all of the credit and part of the blame. The people, the movies, the music, the streets...I want to get it all down and remember it...so I can take it in, digest it and put it behind me. I want to start looking ahead again.)

those two houses down at the end of the street
shared a common back yard...sure, there was a row
of rose bushes separating them, but that was more
decorative than prohibitive.

looking toward the back, toward the tar pit and the
factory, the one on the right had a great big cherry
tree smack dab in the middle. someone, probably
my uncle, at some point built a bench that went all
the way around it. a white bench that was rotted at
the feet and also at the point where it touched up
against the tree.

the yard also had a white cinder block fireplace at
the back.

the fence, such as it was, was chicken wire and kept
nothing out and held nothing in.

there was a gap in the fence for a car to pull in, and
no fence at all where the rose bushes were, creating
(like i said) more or less one great big yard.

memory's a funny thing.

when i think of my aunts and uncles, on both sides,
in both houses, i think of them like old
photographs...some, in black and white, like the

movies we saw then and the ones we grew up
on...and in color, like Polaroids...all cracked now,
and fading away, but back then pointing clearly to
the future.

in those photos, i can still see the yards. i can still
make out their faces. i can put names to the faces
and sometimes even dates.

but, their voices are gone.

they're all dead now and i'm all they got left to
keep a certain part of them alive.

they were World War II people.

Tom Brokaw called them "The Greatest
Generation." he even wrote a book about them and
made a lot of money telling their stories...how they
lived and how they died. but, even that book was
years ago, and the last time i saw Brokaw anywhere
he looked old and tired and nearly done himself.

life has a way of doing that.

like i said...their voices are all gone now, and for
some strange reason, when i think back to them, it's
the voices i remember most. whenever the family

got together there were songs. always singing.
songs that were old when even *they* were young.
songs from the early 1900's...Tin Pan Alley...the
Gibson Girl.

Down By The Old Mill Stream...
Peg Of My Heart...

i can hear them harmonizing right now:

> *"i love you as I loved you when you were sweeeet*
> *sixteen!"*

what was it *they* were looking for? hell..*they* had
fought and won the war. *they* had all the answers.
could they possibly have been looking back over
their shoulders the same way i am now? as simple
and stupid as it may seem…that thought blows me
away.

could my grandmother, across the street from
us...could *she* (in her long printed dress and black
boxer's shoes) be thinking back to something so far
in her past that i couldn't even imagine it?

when she sat there in her parlor, praying the rosary,
in her chair at the back of the room, did her mind
sometimes wander back to days in Poland when

she was a girl? could she have untold
Raskolnikov's in her past? did she pray her rosary
for forgiveness for something she may have done?

what guilt and sadness could she harbor?

and my grandfather? what about him? what could
he have done to make him sit so quiet in the
kitchen all those years?

my mind reels at the thought, and it's safer to think
back to that cookout and those houses down the
street. at least my parents and their dreams and
their memories weren't so very far removed from
mine.

IV

but, i can't seem to get my grandmother off my
mind.

that's just the way she was...a short, quietly
commanding woman, with impossibly grey hair
pulled back in a bun.

i don't ever remember seeing her with her hair any
other way except pulled back really tight and
severe in that bun, held in place with these little
tiny bobby pins that she kept in a little plastic case,
on the table next to the chair where she sat.

the only time i ever saw her with her hair down
was years later...my grandfather was already dead
and she was living with one of her kids...

i remember she walked into the kitchen, in that
house (it was morning then) and her hair was
down, and i was shocked to see how long and thin
it was...it came all the way down to her waist, and
for some reason it made her look even shorter.

when she walked into the room to see me and my
then brand new wife, she came up to me, hugged
me and smiled. i thought "who *is* this woman? my

grandmother never smiles. she never stands like that!"

i never saw her hands, except when she was rolling dough, or praying, holding her rosary and mouthing the words as if to let the world know she was deep in prayer and talking to god.

(Note to self: I can't remember ever seeing her shopping. I'm sure she went. She had to. Dad must have taken her downtown in our old '57 Chevy. Or, later, in the '62 that my sister named "The Great Brown Bomb Bruce." Maybe I was just too young to remember.)

getting back to that room where my grandmother sat and prayed, there was a window directly behind her. she used to tell me that when her eyes got tired from reading her bible she'd pull up the blinds and look out the window...out, across the low land that flooded so bad in '72...out, toward the hills in the distance. she said it was good for her eyes...and she'd rub them, put her glasses on and go back to her book...that bible with the black cover, embossed with the cross...and the red pages.

the red

pages

if you looked out that window...just before the tracks...just before the land sloped down to where the flood was in '72, there were two white houses, separated by a great big plot of land where we played football in the fall.

tackle football.

looking back, the yard wasn't very big, but, neither were we. that didn't stop us from having what we thought were the most amazingly epic football games ever.

we played, and we played *hard*.

we held absolutely nothing back. if somebody got tackled really hard and got the wind knocked out of him it was cause for celebration.

did you ever have the wind knocked out of you? it hurts like hell and it's scary. but, if it happens often enough, you eventually learn that if you stay calm and wait it out, things will come back to normal, and you can get on with the game.

life's kinda like that. i didn't know it then, but i
know it now.

back then we were just having fun, and if it
sometimes meant rolling around on the ground,
going blue in the face, that's just the way it was.
it was all a part of the fun.

V

there was a Greek family who lived around the
corner from there...out near the tracks. in the
summer the old man used to sit on his porch and
watch us kids playing cork ball in the street.

it was a version of stick ball that we played with a
cork...a small barrel-shaped cork that we used to
get up at the sporting good's store in the fishing
department. we'd wrap it real tight with electrical
tape so it wouldn't fall apart, and if you knew what
you were doing, a good pitcher could make that
thing curve a good 3 feet or drop and dip and even
rise if you held it right and threw it hard enough.
the stick was just an old broom handle that we got
from somewhere in the house.

i don't think we ever talked to the old man. i don't
even know if he knew English, but he was our
audience, and we were the only game in town.

once a year the Greeks would have a great big
party. and that year (the only year i have any
memory of) they had cars and trucks parked all
over the place while they were getting ready. they
were parked in the street, out on the lawn and in
the back yard.

we were fascinated.

i don't think any of them spoke English. i don't remember hearing it. they were the most exotic thing we'd ever seen.

it never occurred to us that we all had parents or grandparents who spoke Polish or Slovak or Lithuanian. but, for us, this was a big deal. a very big deal.

and when we heard that a pig got loose, and was running all over the neighborhood, we dropped whatever it was we were doing and started to give chase.

the pig ran wild, in and out of yards, and while we had always heard of greased pig contests, and had even seen one in a movie or two, this was our very own chance at having the real thing.

the neighborhood was in an uproar...kids were yelling...moms and dads were out on porches (this had to have been a saturday, because there *were* dads out and about...i'm sure of it)...even Mrs. Nutchie — who never came outside except to hang clothes on the line or maybe near the 4th of July,

when she and her husband used to sell firecrackers
and things to everyone.

they used to make a trip every year, going out to
New Jersey or somewhere where fireworks were
legal...across the state line and they'd sell us
anything we wanted. everything from bottle
rockets to cherry bombs and flares. we never
bought any flares because my father worked in the
mines and he'd bring home these big long road
flares, as big as sticks of dynamite and on the 4th
we'd light them in the front yard and they glowed a
bright wild orange.

yeah, everyone was out and we chased that pig all
over the place, getting our hands on
it...diving...sliding...having it get away...until we
finally got the best of it and brought it back, taking
it into the yard where the Greeks were waiting for
us.

and almost before we knew what had happened,
the grandfather pulled out a knife and cut its
throat.

it stood there, for a second, not even
squealing...blood gushing...looking kinda

surprised. and then one of the men pulled out a pistol and shot it right in the head.

just a little pop. not half as loud as anything Mrs. Nutchie ever sold.

just this little pop, and that was it.

the little pig collapsed into a pool of its own red blood and died.

VI

Dick Tiger died in 1972.

Emile Griffith passed away 42 years later.

VII

(Note to self: Satchel Paige had it right...he once said "don't look back...something might be gaining on you.")

About John Yamrus

Since 1970 John Yamrus has published 25 volumes of poetry and 2 novels. He has also had more than 1,900 poems published in print magazines around the world. Selections of his poetry have been translated into several languages, including Spanish, Swedish, French, Japanese, Italian, Romanian, Albanian and most recently Bengali. His poetry is taught in several colleges and universities. His website is www.johnyamrus.com.

Also by John Yamrus

As Real As Rain
I Admit Nothing
Burn
Endure
Alchemy
Bark
They Never Told Me This Would Happen
Can't Stop Now!
Doing Cartwheels On Doomsday Afternoon
New And Selected Poems
Blue Collar
Shoot The Moon
One Step at a Time
78 RPM
Keep The Change
New And Used
Start To Finish
Someone Else's Dreams (novel)
Something
Poems
Those
Coming Home
American Night
15 Poems
Heartsongs
Lovely Youth (novel)
I Love

Epic Rites Press